# Parrot Crackers

## Kelly Doudna

Illustrated by Anne Haberstroh

Consulting Editor, Diane Craig, M.A./Reading Specialist

ABDO
Publishing Company

Published by ABDO Publishing Company, 4940 Viking Drive, Edina, Minnesota 55435.

Printed in the United States.

Credits
Edited by: Pam Price
Curriculum Coordinator: Nancy Tuminelly
Cover and Interior Design and Production: Mighty Media
Photo Credits: iStockphoto/Robert Appelbaum, iStockphoto/Christina Craft, iStockphoto/Daniel Defabio, iStockphoto/Mike Pluth, ShutterStock

Library of Congress Cataloging-in-Publication Data

Doudna, Kelly, 1963-
    Parrot crackers / Kelly Doudna; illustrated by Anne Haberstroh.
        p. cm. -- (Fact & fiction. Critter chronicles)
    Summary: Peg Leg Polly and her pirate crew capture a cargo of fancy snack crackers--in exchange for some fruit--and bring it to an orphanage. Alternating pages provide facts about different types of parrots.
    ISBN 10  1-59928-458-8 (hardcover)
    ISBN 10  1-59928-459-6 (paperback)

    ISBN 13  978-1-59928-458-3 (hardcover)
    ISBN 13  978-1-59928-459-0 (paperback)
    [1. Pirates--Fiction. 2. Generosity--Fiction. 3. Parrots--Fiction.] I. Haberstroh, Anne, ill. II. Title. III. Series.

    PZ7.D74425Par 2007
    [E]--dc22
                                                                    2006005547

## SandCastle Level: Fluent

SandCastle™ books are created by a professional team of educators, reading specialists, and content developers around five essential components—phonemic awareness, phonics, vocabulary, text comprehension, and fluency—to assist young readers as they develop reading skills and strategies and increase their general knowledge. All books are written, reviewed, and leveled for guided reading, early reading intervention, and Accelerated Reader® programs for use in shared, guided, and independent reading and writing activities to support a balanced approach to literacy instruction. The SandCastle™ series has four levels that correspond to early literacy development. The levels help teachers and parents select appropriate books for young readers.

**Emerging Readers**
(no flags)

**Beginning Readers**
(1 flag)

**Transitional Readers**
(2 flags)

**Fluent Readers**
(3 flags)

These levels are meant only as a guide. All levels are subject to change.

# FACT & Fiction

This series provides early fluent readers the opportunity to develop reading comprehension strategies and increase fluency. These books are appropriate for guided, shared, and independent reading.

**FACT** The left-hand pages incorporate realistic photographs to enhance readers' understanding of informational text.

**Fiction** The right-hand pages engage readers with an entertaining, narrative story that is supported by whimsical illustrations.

The Fact and Fiction pages can be read separately to improve comprehension through questioning, predicting, making inferences, and summarizing. They can also be read side-by-side, in spreads, which encourages students to explore and examine different writing styles.

**FACT** OR **Fiction?** This fun quiz helps reinforce students' understanding of what is real and not real.

**SPEED READ** The text-only version of each section includes word-count rulers for fluency practice and assessment.

**GLOSSARY** Higher-level vocabulary and concepts are defined in the glossary.

## SandCastle™ would like to hear from you.

Tell us your stories about reading this book. What was your favorite page? Was there something hard that you needed help with? Share the ups and downs of learning to read. To get posted on the ABDO Publishing Company Web site, send us an e-mail at:

**sandcastle@abdopublishing.com**

Parrots live in the warm parts of the world.
Parrot species include macaws, cockatoos,
and budgies.

Peg Leg Polly Parrot is captain of the pirate ship *Oyster Shell*. The *Oyster Shell* is anchored near a small island in the tropical ocean.

Parrots hold their food with one foot while they eat. Parrots are either left-footed or right-footed.

"Arrr!" Peg Leg Polly says in her gravelly pirate voice. "The USS *Saltine* will soon be sailing to this side of the island. Then we'll trade our cargo of fruit for the load of fancy snack crackers she'll be carrying today."

Parrots are believed to have intelligence and emotions similar to those of a 3- to 5-year-old human child.

Corky Cockatoo is a brand-new member of the crew, and this is his first mission. He asks, "Then what, Captain? Will we have a feast of crackers at sunset?"

Peg Leg Polly answers, "Arrr! No, matey. We'll donate the loot to the Nest for the Needy so the orphans can have a special treat. Arrr!"

Parrots make a variety of sounds. Wild parrots never mimic, or copy, human speech. Only captive parrots do this.

Corky grumbles to the first mate, Bubba Budgie, "I thought pirates raided for gold and treasure."

Bubba replies, "Not Peg Leg Polly. Her mission is to do good things for others. Look!" Just then, the USS *Saltine* appears in the distance.

At four feet or more, the wingspan of the hyacinth macaw is the greatest of all parrots.

As the *Saltine* passes the island, Bubba and Corky raise the *Oyster Shell's* sails. "Full ahead! Arrr!" Peg Leg Polly commands. In no time, the *Oyster Shell* catches up to the *Saltine*.

13

Macaws and cockatoos might fly as much as 500 miles per day in search of food.

Peg Leg Polly
and her crew load
crates and crates of fancy
snack crackers onto the *Oyster
Shell.* Then they fill the cargo hold
of the *Saltine* with fruit and speed
away in the opposite direction.

**15**

Parrots live in flocks. They nest in tree holes, rock cavities, and termite mounds. Very few of the more than 300 species of parrots build stick nests.

NEST for the NEEDY

Peg Leg Polly sails the *Oyster Shell* back to the mainland. At the Nest for the Needy, the orphans are excited to see the pirates because they always bring something good.

17

The life spans of parrots vary. Larger macaws and cockatoos can live for 75 years or longer.

Peg Leg Polly, Bubba, and Corky watch as the orphans enjoy the fancy snack crackers. Peg Leg Polly says, "Arrr, mateys. Just look at the smiles on their wee faces! It's time to go. Our next mission awaits!"

# FACT OR FiCTiON?

Read each statement below. Then decide whether it's from the FACT section or the FiCTiON section!

1. Parrots sail pirate ships.

2. Parrots hold their food with one foot.

3. Parrots donate food to orphans.

4. Parrots nest in tree holes.

Parrots live in the warm parts of the world. Parrot 10

species include macaws, cockatoos, and budgies. 16

Parrots hold their food with one foot while they eat. 26

Parrots are either left-footed or right-footed. 34

Parrots are believed to have intelligence and 41

emotions similar to those of a 3- to 5-year-old human 53

child. 54

Parrots make a variety of sounds. Wild parrots never 63

mimic, or copy, human speech. Only captive parrots 71

do this. 73

At four feet or more, the wingspan of the hyacinth 83

macaw is the greatest of all parrots. 90

Macaws and cockatoos might fly as much as 500 99

miles per day in search of food. 106

Parrots live in flocks. They nest in tree holes, rock 116

cavities, and termite mounds. Very few of the more 125

than 300 species of parrots build stick nests. 133

The life spans of parrots vary. Larger macaws and 142

cockatoos can live for 75 years or longer. 150

**21**

Peg Leg Polly Parrot is captain of the pirate ship *Oyster Shell*. The *Oyster Shell* is anchored near a small island in the tropical ocean. 9 18 25

"Arrr!" Peg Leg Polly says in her gravelly pirate voice. "The USS *Saltine* will soon be sailing to this side of the island. Then we'll trade our cargo of fruit for the load of fancy snack crackers she'll be carrying today." 34 44 54 64 66

Corky Cockatoo is a brand-new member of the crew, and this is his first mission. He asks, "Then what, Captain? Will we have a feast of crackers at sunset?" 75 85 94 96

Peg Leg Polly answers, "Arrr! No, matey. We'll donate the loot to the Nest for the Needy so the orphans can have a special treat. Arrr!" 104 115 122

Corky grumbles to the first mate, Bubba Budgie, "I thought pirates raided for gold and treasure." 129 137 138

**22**

Bubba replies, "Not Peg Leg Polly. Her mission is to do good things for others. Look!" Just then, the USS *Saltine* appears in the distance.

As the *Saltine* passes the island, Bubba and Corky raise the *Oyster Shell*'s sails. "Full ahead! Arrr!" Peg Leg Polly commands. In no time, the *Oyster Shell* catches up to the *Saltine*.

Peg Leg Polly and her crew load crates and crates of fancy snack crackers onto the *Oyster Shell*. Then they fill the cargo hold of the *Saltine* with fruit and speed away in the opposite direction.

Peg Leg Polly sails the *Oyster Shell* back to the mainland. At the Nest for the Needy, the orphans are excited to see the pirates because they always bring something good.

Peg Leg Polly, Bubba, and Corky watch as the orphans enjoy the fancy snack crackers. Peg Leg Polly says, "Arrr, mateys. Just look at the smiles on their wee faces! It's time to go. Our next mission awaits!"

# GLOSSARY

**captive.** kept under another's control

**cargo.** goods carried on a ship, train, or other vehicle

**donate.** to give a gift in order to help others

**emotion.** a feeling such as happiness or sadness

**hold.** the area on a boat or airplane where cargo is stored

**mission.** a special job or assignment

**orphan.** a child who doesn't have any parents

**species.** a group of related living beings

**tropical.** located in the hottest areas on earth

**wingspan.** the distance from one wing tip to the other when the wings are fully spread

To see a complete list of SandCastle™ books and other nonfiction titles from ABDO Publishing Company, visit www.abdopublishing.com or contact us at: 4940 Viking Drive, Edina, Minnesota 55435 • 1-800-800-1312 • fax: 1-952-831-1632